MW00949292

Octo and Nim

Written by

Johnnie McCorvey

Illustrated by

Carren McDaniel

Copyright © 2016 Johnnie McCorvey

All rights reserved.
ISBN-10: 1523300973
ISBN-13: 978-1523300976

DEDICATION

This book is dedicated to my two beautiful daughters Makenna and Caton.

May our differences shine and make us better people..

This book belongs to

Kaylee
_____

dream, study hard
read and listen
to your parents

It was early September and summer was coming to an end. Soon it would be winter and the ladybugs will go into hibernation, as the days will be dark and cold. Today, it was a sunny and warm day and all the children were playing in the park. There were puppies running through the grass and kittens playing with the fallen leaves.

If one looked closely they could see a very small world.
The world of bugs, beetles and arachnids.

An alien looking black and red Pupa (Baby Ladybug),
named Nim was playing near the large Oak Tree. As Nim
was rolling and tumbling in the grass she heard,

"Hello red bug with black dots."

Nim looked all around and could see nothing. Then straight above her, hanging upside down, suspended in air was a baby spider.

Nim looked at the spider and was frightened.

Nim had six legs and this thing had eight legs. Nim
remembered a story her mother had told her. She told
Nim to stay away from spiders because they are not bugs
and they will eat you. Nim was really scared of this odd
looking arachnid.

The spider shouted, "My name is Octo as I have eight legs and eight eyes."

Soon the two youngsters were talking.

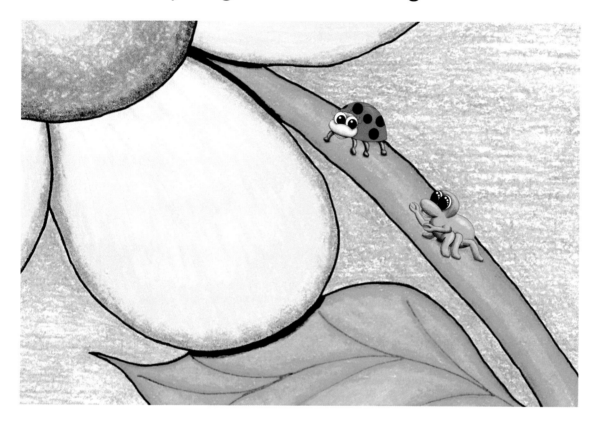

Nim was beginning to like Octo. And Octo liked Nim. They were becoming friends. Octo explained to Nim that there were thousands of different kinds of spiders. Octo was a vegetarian, much like Nim. Octo shared stories of the insect eating spiders. He told her of the hairy Tarantula and the poisonous Black Widow. However,

Octo had no hair like the Tarantula and Octo's stomach did not have the red hour glass tattoo like the Black Widow.

Nim was delighted that she had found a friend. Everyday Nim and Octo would play in the park. They loved each other's company.

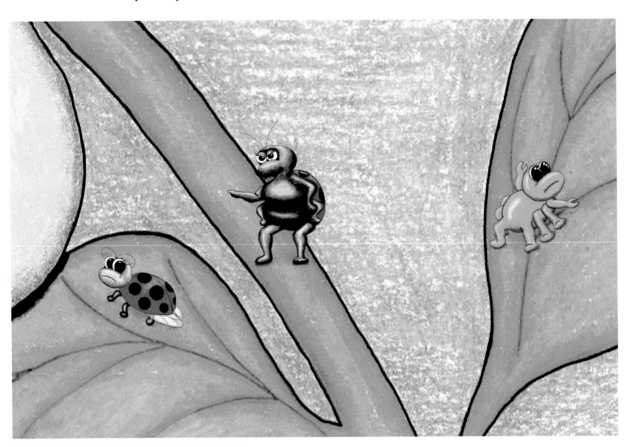

One day Nim's mother saw the two playing together and was outraged. Nim's mother forbid the two to play together. This was a very sad day. Even though

Nim and Octo were different they loved each other.

Seven months had passed and Nim and Octo had gone their separate ways. It was finally Spring, a time of delight. The harsh winter had passed. All of the lady bugs were flying through the blue sky; not a care in the world, flying and flying.

Nim was happily resting on a very high tree branch next
to her mother.

Suddenly above them a very large branch fell. The branch was falling towards Nim and her mother. As the two began to fly away, Nim was struck by the branch, her wing broke from the blow.

As she was falling she grabbed onto a twig that was in her downward path. With her six legs she held tightly onto the twig high above the hard ground. Nim was crying. She was weak and could not hold on long. If she let go she would fall. The lady bugs were flying around and crying, knowing that Nim may die.

No one could survive this fall.

Nim was crying. Octo was near and heard a familiar voice. Suddenly Octo realized that it was the voice of his friend Nim. Octo hurried to Nim. Octo was happy to see his old friend. Nim was crying and knew she would soon fall.

Octo looked at Nim and said, "Hang on my friend." Octo hurried down the tree in search of a place to build a web. At the last two feet from the ground, Octo started building a silk web. In minutes the web was built.

Octo hurried up the tree to Nim. Octo told Nim, "We will jump together. We will jump into my web."

Nim replied, " No Octo, I do not want you to hurt yourself." Just then Octo grabbed Nim and jumped. They whirled and twirled down and down. They were screaming as all the lady bugs watched.

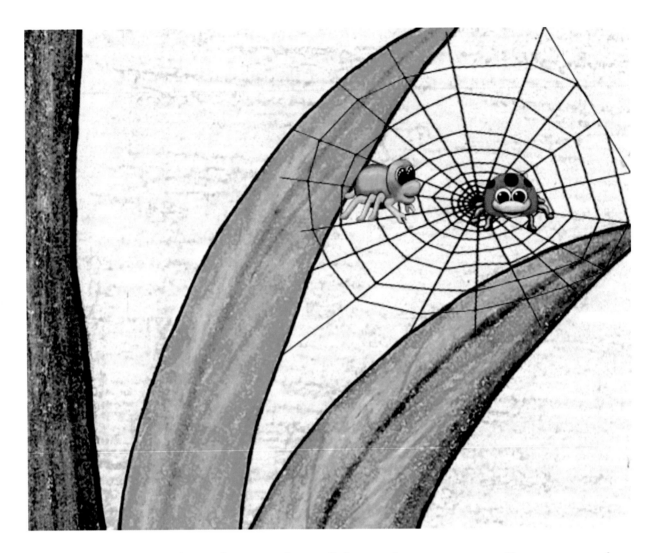

Nim and Octo hit the web softly. There was silence and finally a shout. Nim yelled, "I am okay! I was saved by my friend!" The other lady bugs were happy and could not believe what they had seen. The lady bugs could not believe what had happened.

From that day forward Octo was known as a friend to all ladybugs. The moral of the story is;

Even though we are different, we can still be friends.

ABOUT THE AUTHOR

Johnnie, author and educator. He volunteers his time with Camp Taylor, a cost free medically supervised camp for Children with Heart Defects.

ABOUT THE ILLUSTRATOR

Carren, artist and educator lives in the beautiful San Joaquin Valley of California. She is active in animal rescue. More information about her work can be found at www.creativecarren.com

Made in the USA
Monee, IL
22 March 2021

62506169R10017